To Mr Patterson,
best school shows ever!
R.P.

First published 2013 by Macmillan Children's Books
an imprint of Pan Macmillan
The Smithson, 6 Briset Street, London EC1M 5NR
EU representative: Macmillan Publishers Ireland Limited, 1st Floor,
The Liffey Trust Centre, 117-126 Sheriff Street Upper, Dublin 1, D01 YC43
Associated companies throughout the world
www.panmacmillan.com

ISBN: 978-1-4472-2019-0

Text and illustrations copyright © Rebecca Patterson 2013
Moral rights asserted.

9

A CIP catalogue record for this book is available
from the British Library.

Printed in China.

FSC
www.fsc.org

MIX
Paper | Supporting
responsible forestry
FSC® C116313

Angel
Song

Rebecca Patterson

The CHRISTMAS SHOW

MACMILLAN CHILDREN'S BOOKS

We are putting on a Christmas Show!

CHRISTMAS POEMS YEAR 1

Joe

I wasn't listening when
Miss Bright gave out
the parts,

so I don't know
what I am.

Ashton and
Claudia are
the BIG parts,

and Connor
is the triangle.

I know I'm not
a narrator,

or a recorder.

I'm meant to
sing a bit,

but when did we all learn THIS song?

I'm not the
Important Angel,

or a King.

I'm not even in the Donkey Dance!

So in this show I think I am almost . . .

nothing.

But then Miss Bright gives me a
tea towel for my head and tells
me I'm a shepherd!

We practise all afternoon.
It takes a long time!

And now it's Thursday. The Big Day!

Remember
No SHOW + TELL on Thursday

The Angel Came down and Said

We miss Show and Tell
so we can get ready.

It is almost time for
our show! The Baby
Jesus is ready,

the Angel has brushed her hair,

and one of the
recorders has a
tummyache.

EVERYONE is here!

We all go
on stage -
quietly, with no
pushing please!

And the show begins.

I think it is going well, until . . .

I sing in the
WRONG BIT!

Then I sing in the right bit but
dance the WRONG WAY!

I forget to go off,

and the
Important Angel
has to WAIT!

After the show, the Angel says SOME
people should NOT be in shows AT ALL!

But I don't care . . .

. . . because my Granny says
I was the BEST THING in it!